To my parents, who got who I was,
and got me the dolls I asked for.

And to Mary Anne Davis, who took Little Bob
to her heart and suggested the above dedication.
With gratitude and love
J. H.

For Marie, my super-duper sister!
Thank you for being you xxx
L. E. A.

Text copyright © 2016 by James Howe
Illustrations copyright © 2016 by Laura Ellen Anderson

First edition 2016

Library of Congress Catalog Card Number pending
ISBN 978-0-7636-4436-9

16 17 18 19 20 21 CCP 10 9 8 7 6 5 4 3 2 1

Printed in Shenzhen, Guangdong, China

This book was typeset in Berkeley.
The illustrations were created digitally.

Candlewick Press
99 Dover Street
Somerville, Massachusetts 02144

visit us at www.candlewick.com

BIG BOB,
Little Bob

James Howe

illustrated by Laura Ellen Anderson

CANDLEWICK PRESS

When **Big Bob** moved in next door, Little Bob's mother said, "Isn't that nice! You will have someone new to play with. He even has the same name as you!"

To Little Bob, their name was the only thing about them that was the same.
For one thing, Big Bob was big. And Little Bob was, well, little.

But how big or how little they were didn't matter to Little Bob. What mattered was what they liked to *do*.

"Boys do not play with dolls," said Big Bob. "They play with trucks."

"I do not like trucks," said Little Bob. "They are too noisy."

One day, when Little Bob was teaching his students their letters . . .

"I'm sorry," Big Bob said. "You were supposed to catch the ball."

"I'm not very good at catching," said Little Bob.

"Then you can throw and I'll catch," Big Bob said.

Little Bob shook his head.
"I'm not very good at throwing either."

No matter what they did, Big Bob and Little Bob did not do it the same.

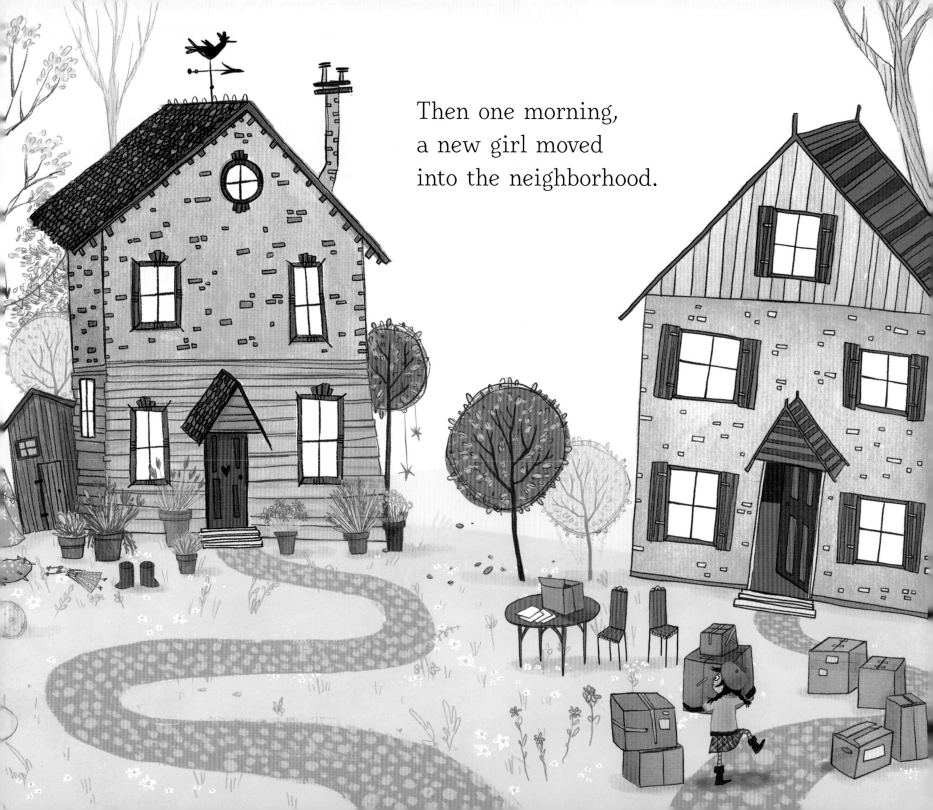

Then one morning,
a new girl moved
into the neighborhood.

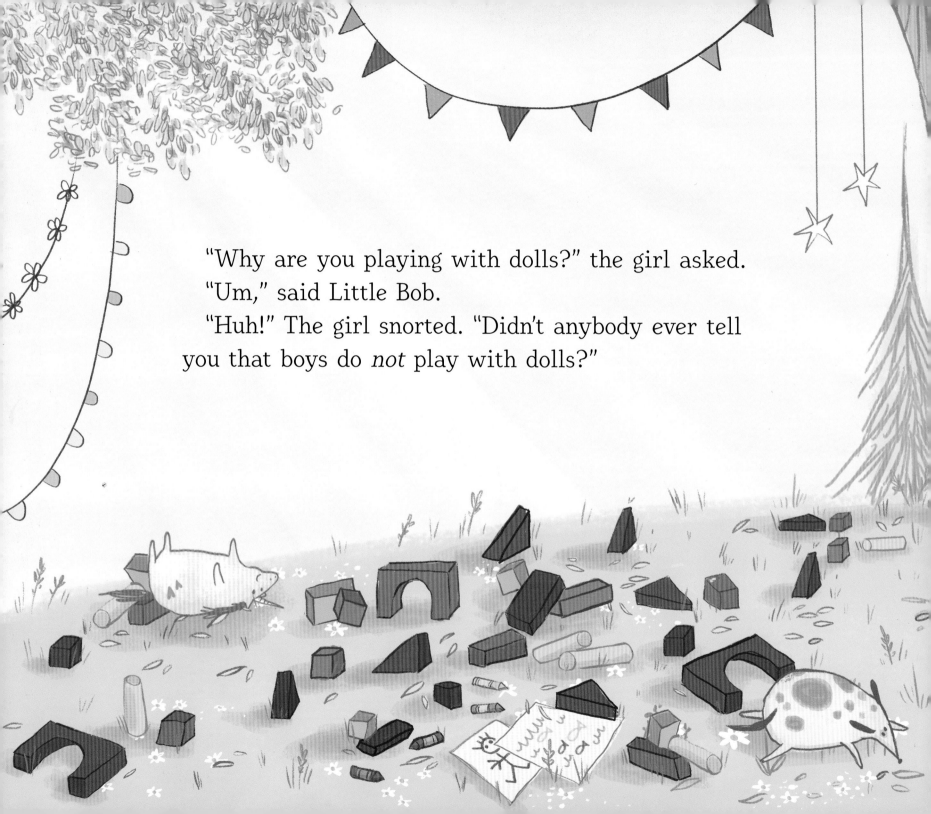

"Why are you playing with dolls?" the girl asked.

"Um," said Little Bob.

"Huh!" The girl snorted. "Didn't anybody ever tell you that boys do *not* play with dolls?"

"Hey! You stop picking on my friend!" Big Bob told
the girl. "Boys can do whatever they want!"

The girl put her head down and turned away.
"Wait!" Little Bob said. "What's your name?"

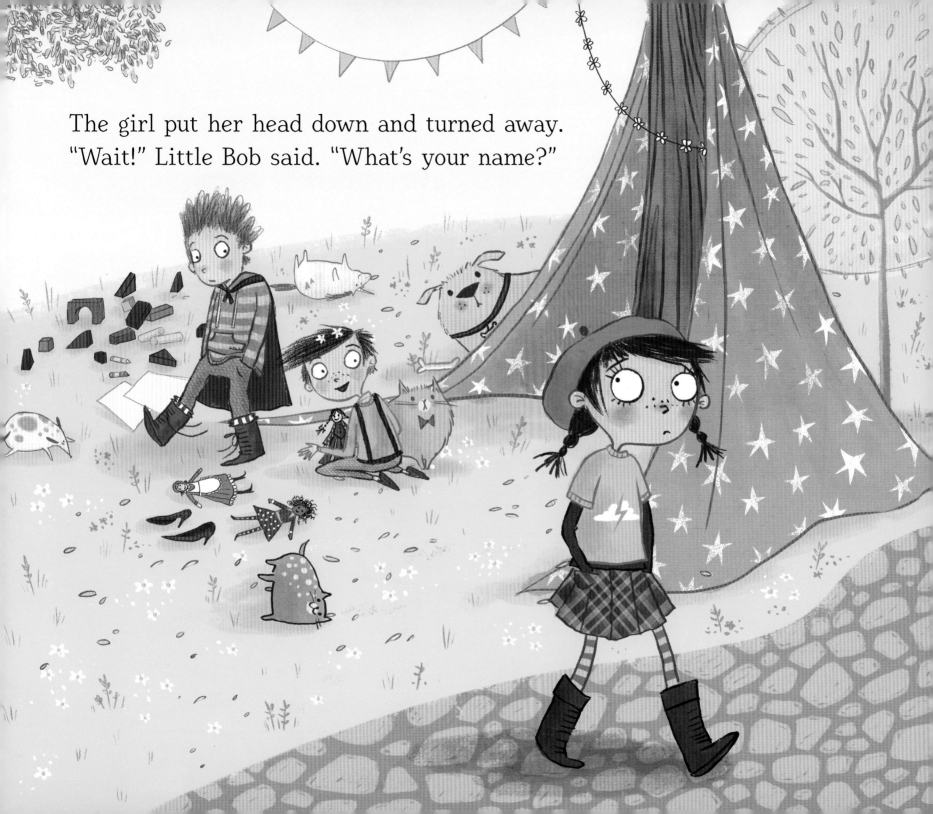

"Blossom," the girl said. "I just moved in next door."
"Do you want to play with us?" Little Bob asked.

"Okay," said Blossom. "But I like playing with trucks more than dolls."

"That's all right," said Big Bob. "Girls can do whatever they want, too."

The three friends played together from that day on.

Big Bob . . . Little Bob . . . and Blossom.